If You're Afraid of the Dark ...

Dedicated to the memory of John Lennon

First Chronicle Books LLC edition published in 2002

Library of Congress Cataloging-in-Publication data:

Edens, Cooper.
     If you're afraid of the dark, remember the night rainbow / by Cooper Edens.
          p.   cm.
     Summary: Presents advice for a variety of situations, including what to do if the sky
        falls, the bus doesn't come, the sun never shines again, and there is no happy ending.
     ISBN 0-8118-3511-1
     [1. Imagination—Fiction. 2. Problem solving—Fiction.]

     PZ7.E223 If 2002
     [E]---dc21   2001047567

Designed by Melissa Passehl Design

Typeset in Goudy
Manufactured in China

Distributed in Canada by Raincoast Books
9050 Shaughnessy Street
Vancouver, BC V6P 6E5

10 9 8 7 6 5 4 3 2 1

Chronicle Books LLC
85 Second Street
San Francisco, California 94105
www.chroniclebooks.com

If You're Afraid of the Dark

Remember the Night Rainbow

By Cooper Edens

CHRONICLE BOOKS

SAN FRANCISCO

If tomorrow morning the sky falls

have clouds for breakfast.

If night falls

use stars for streetlights.

If the moon gets stuck in a tree

cover the hole in the sky with a strawberry.

If you have butterflies in your stomach

ask them into your heart.

If your heart catches in your throat

ask a bird how she sings.

If the birds forget their songs

listen to a pebble instead.

If you lose a memory

embroider a new one to take its place.

If you lose the key

throw away the house.

If the clock stops

use your own hands to tell time.

If the light goes out

wear it around your neck and go dancing.

If the bus doesn't come

       catch a fast cloud.

If it's the last dance

  dance backwards.

If you find your socks don't match

       stand in a flowerbed.

If your shoes don't fit

give them to the fish in the pond.

If your horse needs shoes

let him use his wings.

If the sun never shines again

hold fireflies in your hands to keep warm.

If you're afraid of the dark

remember the night rainbow.

If there is no happy ending

make one out of cookie dough.